MAÑANA, IGUANA

by

ANN WHITFORD PAUL

illustrated by

ETHAN LONG

SCHOLASTIC INC.

New York Toronto London Auckland Sydney
Mexico City New Delhi Hong Kong Buenos Aires

For Jon,
who rarely puts anything off until *mañana*
A. W. P.

For Rosemary and Bob
E. L.

ISBN 0-439-75663-4

Text copyright © 2004 by Ann Whitford Paul.
Illustrations copyright © 2004 by Ethan Long. All rights reserved.
Published by Scholastic Inc., 557 Broadway, New York, NY 10012,
by arrangement with Holiday House, Inc. SCHOLASTIC and associated logos
are trademarks and/or registered trademarks of Scholastic Inc.

12 11 10 9 8 7 6 5 4 3 2 1   5 6 7 8 9 10/0

Printed in the U.S.A.   40

First Scholastic printing, May 2005

The text typeface is Barcelona.
The artwork was created with watercolors and gouache on watercolor paper.

GLOSSARY

The days of the week

lunes	LOON es	Monday
martes	MART es	Tuesday
miércoles	me AIR co les	Wednesday
jueves	WEV es	Thursday
viernes	vee AIR nes	Friday
sábado	SAH bid o	Saturday
domingo	doe MING o	Sunday

Other words in Spanish

conejo	co NAY ho	rabbit
culebra	cu LAY brah	snake
fiesta	fee EST ah	party
gracias	GRAH see us	thank you
mañana	mun YAHN ah	tomorrow
piñata	pin YAH tah	name of a container filled with candy or toys that is broken with a stick at parties
tortuga	tor TU gah	tortoise
yo no	yo NO	not I
yo sí	yo SEE	I will

On Monday, *lunes*, Iguana twitched her tail happily.
"Let's celebrate spring with a party on Saturday."
Conejo hopped up and down. "Yes! Let's!"
Tortuga poked out of his shell.
"A *fiesta*? On *sábado*? Count me in."
Culebra shook his rattle. "Me too!"
"Good!" said Iguana. "We must start right away.
Who will help me write the invitations?"

"*Yo no.* Not I," said Conejo.
"I write too fast.
No one could read my words."

"*Yo no,*" said Tortuga.
"I write too slow."

"I can't hold a pen," said Culebra.
"Maybe I'll grow arms tonight
and can help you tomorrow."

"We can't wait until *mañana*."
Iguana wriggled her tail.
"I'll write the invitations
myself."

And she did.

On *martes*, Iguana asked,
"Who will help me deliver
the invitations
for our *fiesta*?"

"*Yo no*," said Conejo.
"I move too fast.
   I'd pass our friends."

"*Yo no*," said Tortuga.
"I move too slow."

Culebra said, "If I grow arms tonight,
I'll help you *mañana*, Iguana."

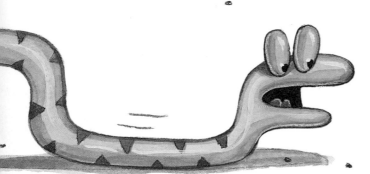

"*Mañana* will be too late."
   Iguana fidgeted her tail.
"I'll deliver the invitations myself."

And she did.

On *miércoles*, Iguana asked,
"Who will help me stuff the *piñata* for our *fiesta*?"

"*Yo no,*" said Conejo.
"I stuff too fast. I'd rip and tear."

"*Yo no,*" said Tortuga. "I stuff too slow."

Culebra said, "*Mañana,* Iguana,
when I grow arms."

"Too many excuses!"
Iguana flounced her tail.
"I'll stuff the *piñata* myself!"

And she did.

On *jueves*, Iguana begged, "Please, will someone help me cook the food for our *fiesta*?"

"*Yo no*," said Conejo. "I cook too fast. I'd make a mess."
"*Yo no*," said Tortuga. "I cook too slow."
Culebra said, "If I grow arms, I'll help you
mañana, Iguana."
Iguana slapped her tail on the ground.
"I'll cook the food myself!"

And she did.

On *viernes*, Iguana sighed.
"I don't suppose anyone will help me hang the streamers for our *fiesta*."

"*Yo no,*" said Conejo.
"I hang too fast. I'd tear the streamers."
"*Yo no,*" said Tortuga. "I hang too slow."
Culebra said, "I'll help you hang the streamers."

Iguana clapped.
"Hurray!"

"I'll help you *mañana*, Iguana, when I grow my arms."

"I knew it!"
Iguana smacked her tail
on the ground so hard,
she puffed up a cloud of dirt.
"I'll decorate by myself!"

And she did.

And then it was *sábado*.

Conejo hopped up and down. "We're ready for our *fiesta*."

Tortuga poked out of his shell. "Here come our guests."

Culebra shook his rattle. "Let's greet them."

"No!"

Iguana whipped her tail around in angry circles.
"I wrote the invitations, and I delivered them.
I stuffed the *piñata.* I cooked the food.
I hung the streamers. Now I, and I alone,
will greet my guests at my fiesta."

And she did.

Conejo hurried to hide behind a cactus.
Tortuga shrunk into his shell.
Culebra slithered under a rock.

They watched
for a long time
while the guests
laughed and ate
and broke the *piñata*.

"What a fine *fiesta!*" the guests said as they left.

Iguana yawned.
"I'm too tired to clean up. I'll do it *mañana*."
She stretched out and soon slept.

Conejo hopped out
from behind the cactus.
"Iguana's really worn out,"
he said.

Tortuga poked
out of his shell.
"She should be.
She did everything."

Culebra slithered out
from under the rock.
"And *we* did *nothing*!"

They were silent
for a long time.

Suddenly Conejo said, "I have an idea."
He told it to his friends.
"That's great!" said Tortuga.
Culebra said, "Let's start now!"

And they did.

Conejo pulled down streamers,
put away leftovers,
and packed up trash.

Tortuga scrubbed, and scrubbed, and scrubbed one giant platter.

And Culebra squiggled and squirmed,
sweeping the ground spotless.

They worked until *domingo,* and Iguana woke up.
She rubbed her eyes and looked around.
She looked at Conejo, and Tortuga, and Culebra.
Iguana smiled.
"*¡Gracias!*" she said. "Thank you."

Then she twitched her tail happily.
"You must be hungry from your hard work.
Who will help me eat the leftovers?"
"¡*Yo sí!*" cried Conejo, Tortuga, and Culebra.

And they **all** did.